Table of Contents

Endless Paths: The Choose-Your-Own Doom Chronicles (Retro Horrors: The Lost Decade) 1

Chapter 1: 5
Chapter 2: 11
Chapter 3: 17
Chapter 4: 23
Chapter 5: 29
Chapter 6: 35
Chapter 7: 41
Chapter 8: 45
Chapter 9: 53
Chapter 10: 59
Chapter 11: 65
Chapter 12: 71
Chapter 13: 77

Dedicated *To You. May you always find a reason to smile!*

Endless Paths:
The Choose-Your-Doom Chronicles
A Retro Horrors: The Lost Decade Book
By: B. Humphrey

Contents

Chapter 1:
Chapter 2:
Chapter 3:
Chapter 4:
Chapter 5:
Chapter 6:
Chapter 7:
Chapter 8:
Chapter 9:
Chapter 10:
Chapter 11:
Chapter 12:
Chapter 13:

Chapter 1:

The bell above the door jingled, echoing through the cramped aisles of *Whisper Pages*. The air inside was thick with the scent of dust, old paper, and something faintly metallic, like a coin forgotten in the bottom of a drawer. Jordan stepped through the doorway, wiping rain off his jacket sleeve, and took a deep breath. This place was the closest thing to time travel in their small town, and Jordan loved every second of it.

He ran a hand through his messy dark hair and adjusted his backpack strap. His shoes squelched slightly against the uneven wooden floor as he glanced around. Somewhere between the tall stacks of old hardcovers and yellowed comic books, he hoped he'd find the weird treasure he'd been craving, a strange book, something no one else would care about but would eat up hours of his time.

The store's owner, Mr. Ellington, sat behind the counter, flipping through a worn National Geographic. He looked like a skeleton dressed up for a party; skin stretched too thin over a narrow face, with deep-set eyes peeking over the rims of glasses that balanced precariously on his nose. When Jordan entered, Mr. Ellington gave a dry cough, the kind old men made when they wanted to be left alone, and returned to his magazine.

"Yo, Jordan!" A familiar voice called from the back. Jordan grinned, kicking some loose paperback novels out of the way as he walked deeper into the store. "Ash? You hiding in here again?"

Ashley "Ash" Cordero poked her head around a display of vintage Goosebumps books. Her black bangs flopped over her forehead, with a mischievous grin spread across her face. In one hand, she clutched a sketchbook filled with creepy doodles. Ash was the kind of friend who could make anything feel like an adventure, even a slow afternoon in a dusty old bookstore.

"Found anything good?" Jordan asked, scanning the shelves. "Not yet," Ash replied, flipping her sketchbook closed. "But this place is a goldmine. There's gotta be something."

Jordan gave a small grin and wandered off into one of the shadowed aisles. Every shelf felt like it held a secret, stacked with worn sci-fi novels, outdated encyclopedias, and occult manuals. There, tucked in a corner where the light barely reached, he saw a plain black book with no title on the spine.

He hesitated before pulling it out. The book felt cold to the touch, as though it had been left outside in the rain. The cover was matte, with a subtle embossing of strange symbols, circles, arrows, and slashes, like a language Jordan didn't know. He flipped it open to the first page.

"Endless Paths: A Game of Choices"

Jordan's heart gave a little leap. A *Choose-Your-Own-Adventure* book? He loved those. The idea of making choices and seeing the story unfold differently every time was his kind of fun. But this one looked... different. There was something off about the artwork. The illustrations were unnervingly detailed, more lifelike than the cartoons he was used to. One picture showed a small figure standing at the edge of a forest, shadows curling from the trees like hands.

He felt a tap on his shoulder, and Ash leaned over, peeking at the book. "What's that?"

"Found something cool Ash Pazash," Jordan said, grinning. "Looks like a choose-your-own-adventure, but super creepy."

He flipped to another page. This one showed a boy, about his age, staring into a mirror with something wrong in his reflection, his eyes were blackened pits, and behind him, shadows began to take shape.

"Whoa," Ash whispered. "That's kinda weird."

"Let's play it," Jordan said, grinning wider.

Ash raised an eyebrow. "You mean *read* it?"

"Nope. We'll act it out. Like a real adventure. See what choices we get, then we do them. Come on, it'll be fun."

Ash gave him a skeptical look, but Jordan could see the excitement brewing beneath. "You're serious?"

"As serious as an old man trying to return soup at a deli." Jordan tucked the book under his arm. "Let's get Marz and Jenny. We're playing this thing tonight."

By the time Jordan and Ash made it to the playground where their friends were hanging out, the rain had stopped, leaving the metal slide slick and the jungle gym gleaming under the cloudy sky.

"Marz, Jenny! Get over here!" Jordan called, waving the book in the air.

Marcus 'Marz' Whitman jumped off his BMX bike, the wheels skidding slightly on the wet asphalt.

"What's that?" he asked, pushing his curly hair out of his face. He was always the first to dive headfirst into any scheme Jordan cooked up, usually without bothering to ask questions.

Jenny Thompson sat on a bench, fiddling with her Walkman. She glanced up, unimpressed. "Another one of your weirdo ideas, Jordan?" she asked, sliding her headphones off.

"This one's not weird," Jordan said, plopping down next to her. "It's awesome, like me."

He slapped the book on the bench, letting the others gather around. Marz ran his fingers over the cover. "Endless Paths? Is it, like, cursed or something?"

"Maybe," Ash said, grinning. "Guess we'll find out." Jenny sighed, crossing her arms. "If this thing makes us end up in detention again, I swear, I'm never trusting you again."

Jordan opened the book to the first page. "Okay, here's how it works. We read the choices out loud, and whatever we pick, we have to do. Simple."

"What's the worst that could happen?" Marz asked.

The first page offered a simple scenario:

"You stand at the entrance of an ancient forest. Do you walk inside (turn to page 13), or go back home (turn to page 7)?"

"Easy," Jordan said, his eyes gleaming. "We walk into the forest."

He flipped to page 13. As he read aloud, the air seemed to shift slightly. The wind picked up, swirling the wet leaves at their feet.

"You step deeper into the forest, the shadows closing in. The path twists ahead, but you can't see where it leads. Something is watching you, just out of sight."

Jordan paused, feeling a strange tingle crawl up his spine. The others shuffled nervously.

"Ayoo, you feel that?" Marz said, his grin faltering.

Before anyone could speak again, the playground's streetlights flickered, once, twice, then went dark. An eerie silence settled over them, as if the world had taken a breath and held it.

Jenny stood, looking around. "Okay, that was weird."

"Probably just a big fat coincidence," Jordan said, though he didn't believe it.

Ash squinted toward the forest at the edge of the park. "Dudes... did that tree just move?"

Everyone turned, and for a moment, the group fell silent. At the edge of the woods, a dark shape shifted between the trees. It was subtle, almost like a trick of the light.

"Come on yous guys," Jordan said, in his best mobster accent. "It's just a game."

"Yeah, but maybe we shouldn't play this one," Jenny whispered.

Marz laughed nervously. "What's the worst that could happen?"

Jordan turned the page.

Chapter 2:

The next evening, Jordan sat cross-legged on the worn carpet of his bedroom, the cursed book *Endless Paths* resting in his lap. Outside, the night was heavy with mist, muffling the sounds of distant cars and the occasional bark of a neighbor's dog. His posters of Ghostbusters, Return of the Jedi, and Duran Duran loomed on his walls, the faint green glow of his digital clock casting strange shadows over them.

Ash sprawled across the bed, flipping through her sketchbook. She'd drawn a rough version of the strange shape they saw in the park, her pen strokes jagged and dark.

"Do you think it was real?" she asked without looking up.

Jordan shrugged, drumming his fingers on the book's spine. "I don't know. But that's why we have to keep going, to find out. I mean, we're not scared, right?"

"Speak for yourself duderonimous," Ash muttered.

Just then, Marz kicked the bedroom door open dramatically, holding a bag of Skittles in one hand and a bottle of Coke in the other.

"I come bearing gifts!" he announced, plopping down on the floor next to Jordan.

His BMX jacket squeaked as he settled in. Jenny followed behind, arms crossed, clearly regretting her decision to join. "This is probably a terrible idea. I can feel it deep down in my left ankle."

Jordan smirked. "You feel everything in your ankles weirdo?"

"About to feel your butt with my foot if you keep it up. She said. "I just think maybe messing with weird books that cause power to go out isn't the best plan."

"Too late for that," Marz said, popping a handful of Skittles into his mouth and letting the colorful juices drip down his chin. "We already started."

Jordan smiled and flipped open the book again. "Alright, let's see what happens next."

The group leaned in as Jordan cleared his throat and began reading.

"THE FOREST GROWS DARKER as you move deeper inside. Branches claw at your clothes, and the path narrows into a thin trail. Suddenly, you hear a sound, something rustling behind you. Do you:

- **Run forward and try to find safety? (Turn to page 22)**
- **Turn back and see what's following you? (Turn to page 17)"**

Ash made a face. "Neither of those sound good." Jenny frowned. "We're seriously going to do this? In real life? Like a bunch of drama students."

"That's the whole point!" Marz said through a mouthful of candy. "It's like... immersive storytelling and stuff and junk."

Jenny rolled her eyes, but she didn't leave. Jordan tapped the book's page.

"Alright, who's in?"

Ash sighed. "If we're going to do it, I say we turn back and see what's following us."

Marz groaned. "Why do the creepy thing? Running forward makes more sense."

"Forward's boring," Ash said, smirking. "We're here for the weird stuff."

Jordan glanced between them. "Alright. Vote time. Ash says we turn back, Marz says run forward. Jenny?"

Jenny threw her hands up. "Ugh. Fine. I vote we turn back. But only so we don't waste the first choice."

Jordan grinned. "That's two for turning back. Sorry, Marz. Creepy thing it is."

He flipped the book to page 17.

"You stop and slowly turn around. The sound behind you gets louder—closer. It's not just rustling; now it sounds like breathing. Heavy, labored breaths, as though something large is following you. And then you see it."

Jordan's voice trailed off, and for a moment, everyone was dead silent.

"A shadow emerges from the trees. Its shape is wrong, tall, but hunched, with limbs too long and thin. Its face... you can't see its face, but you feel its eyes staring through you. It takes a step forward. What do you do?"

Options:

- **Run? (Turn to page 29)**
- **Speak to it? (Turn to page 33)**

The air in the room grew tense. Ash sat up, her eyes wide.

"Okay bros and broetts... I don't think I'm digging this anymore," Jenny muttered. "It feels too real."

"Come on," Jordan whispered, excitement buzzing in his chest. "We've got to keep going. Stop being so soft."

Marz grinned nervously. "Alright, I say we speak to it."

Jenny groaned. "What if something actually shows up? Then who's gonna be the soft one?"

Ash shrugged, though Jordan could see her fingers twitching slightly. "Only one way to find out."

"Speak to it it is," Jordan announced. He turned the page.

"You take a deep breath and speak. 'Who's there?'"

The words left Jordan's lips almost without thinking. He froze, his heart hammering in his chest. At that moment, the room's lights flickered, just like the playground the day before.

Jenny gasped. "Okay, what the f—"

Before she could finish, the window by Jordan's bed rattled violently, as though something outside had slammed against it. They all jumped.

Jordan stood slowly, his breath fogging in the cold air. The room felt different, like the space between the walls had stretched, becoming unfamiliar and disorientating.

He stepped cautiously toward the window, heart thudding in his chest. He could feel his friends' eyes on him, waiting, holding their breath. Jordan peered through the glass.

At first, he saw nothing, just the mist swirling under the streetlight outside. But then, slowly, a shape emerged from the fog. A figure. Tall and hunched. With limbs too long and thin.

Jordan's breath caught in his throat. It was the same shape from the book's illustration.

"It's here," he whispered. The lights flickered again and went out. The room plunged into blackness, and the only sounds were their shallow breaths.

"Jordan!" Ash whispered. "What do we do?" Jordan fumbled with the book, trying to find the next page. His fingers shook as he turned to the new choice:

"You are not alone. Something is with you. To survive, you must make a choice."

Options:

- **Hide in the closet. (Turn to page 41)**
- **Open the window and confront it. (Turn to page 45)**

Jordan's hands trembled. "Closet or window?" he asked quickly, his voice a shaky whisper.

"Closet!" Jenny blurted. "We're not confronting that thing!"

"No way!" Marz argued. "We can't hide like a bunch of wimps! Let's see what it is!"

"Closet," Ash whispered. "Just hide."

Jordan swallowed hard and turned to page 41.

"You dive into the closet, your heart pounding, and close the door behind you. In the darkness, you feel your friends pressed against you, their breathing shallow and panicked. Outside the closet, the door to the room opens slowly with a long, agonizing creak. Something steps inside, dragging its limbs across the floor."

The group sat in the pitch-black room, clinging to every word Jordan read aloud. Then, a noise, a slow, deliberate knock came from just *outside* the closet door. They weren't alone.

Chapter 3:

J ordan held his breath, his hands clammy against the book's pages. In the darkness, he could feel the tension radiating from Ash, Marz, and Jenny, all pressed close together inside the cramped closet.

"Who... who did that?" Jenny whispered, her voice barely audible.

"No one," Jordan whispered. "We're all in here."

The second knock came, louder this time followed by a wet dragging sound. It was slow and deliberate, as if whatever was outside wanted them to know it had found them.

Ash squeezed Jordan's arm. "It's the thing from the book. It's in here."

Marz, ever the thrill-seeker, shifted, making the coat hangers clink together. "Maybe it's just someone messing with us."

"Like whom dillweed?" Jenny whispered harshly. "Your mom?"

"Ugh, hate it when you say whom." Marz whispered. "Makes you sound like some old man."

"Shhh." Jordan swallowed hard and tried to calm his racing thoughts. "We need to stay quiet. Let it think we're not here."

As if on cue the closet door rattled violently, like whatever was on the other side was testing its strength.

Jordan flipped frantically to the next page in *Endless Paths* with shaking fingers, squinting through the dim light of his watch's backlight to read the new passage:

"You have one last choice: Stay silent and hope it leaves (Turn to page 59), or throw open the door and run (Turn to page 64)."

"This isn't fun anymore," Jenny whispered, close to tears.

Jordan gritted his teeth. "We have to choose fast. Stay quiet or run?"

"Stay quiet," Ash whispered urgently. "We can't outrun it. We don't even know what it is."

Marz groaned. "Come on! If we stay in here, it's just gonna get us anyway!"

Jenny bit her lip so hard it looked like she might cry. "I don't care what we do, just pick something!"

Jordan inhaled sharply, weighing his options. "Alright," he whispered. "We stay quiet."

With a deep breath, Jordan turned to page 59.

"You huddle in silence like little babies, heart pounding in your chest. The door rattles again, harder this time, but you don't move. You don't breathe. The presence outside the door pauses for a long, agonizing moment... and then, with a low, inhuman groan, it retreats."

"Well I'll be a goats earlobe," Marz whispered, half in disbelief. "It worked."

Ash slumped against the wall of the closet. "I thought we were dead."

Jordan's hands were still trembling as he closed the book for a moment to catch his breath. Then, something changed. The air grew thick and heavy, and the door to the closet creaked open, by itself.

Every nerve in Jordan's body screamed at him to run, but he stayed frozen. Outside the closet, the room had transformed. His posters were gone, the bed was missing, and the walls were stripped bare. The only thing left was a faint glow coming from the open *Endless Paths* book, that was somehow now lying on the floor in the middle of the room.

"What happened to your room Cuz?" Jenny stammered.

"How the hell did the book get out there?" Ash asked, her voice quivering.

"Holy shit Bruh, I think we're inside the book." Marz said as he stepped cautiously out of the closet, looking around with wide eyes. "Okay, this is next-level freaky."

Jordan knew, deep down, that they were no longer in his bedroom. They had crossed into something else, somewhere in between the real world and the one inside the cursed pages.

"We need to finish the game," Jordan whispered. "That's the only way out."

Jenny's eyes narrowed. "And what if we lose?"

No one answered. Jordan bent down and picked up the glowing book from the floor. A new passage had appeared, shimmering faintly on the page:

"The house you are in now belongs to the shadows. If you want to leave, you must finish what you started. But beware—choices will come faster now. If you hesitate, the house will claim you. If you don't finish, you'll be here forever."

"Ah man. See I told you this was bullshit." Ash whispered.

"Yeah, maybe you're right," Jordan replied. "But we gotta finish now."

Marz gave a shaky laugh. "Man, this is just like one of those weird VHS board games... except, you know, not fun."

Jordan turned to the next page. It showed an illustration of the room they were standing in, exact right down to the glowing book in Jordan's hands.

Below it was another set of options:

"A door appears on the wall. Do you:

- **Open it and walk through? (Turn to page 72)**
- **Stay in the room and search for clues? (Turn to page 80)"**

A soft *click* echoed through the room as a door materialized on the far wall, right where the book had said it would. It was old and wooden, with a brass knob that gleamed faintly in the dim light.

Jenny stepped back, her face pale. "It's like the Time Bandits."

Marz leaned in. "Yes! Return the map, Return what you have stolen from me." He echoed in his best Time Bandits voice. "Let's see where it goes."

Ash looked around the room. "We need clues. We should stay here and figure out what this place is."

Jenny crossed her arms. "Yeah, what if we open the door and it traps us?"

Jordan ran a hand through his hair, glancing nervously between his friends. Every instinct screamed that neither option was safe. But he had to choose.

"Alright," Jordan whispered. "We search for clues."

He flipped to page 80.

"You stay in the room, searching every corner for something useful. Under a floorboard, you find an object wrapped in cloth. When you open it, a small, silver key gleams in the low light. But just as you pocket the key, the door behind you swings open with a deafening crash. Something has found you."

Before anyone could react, the wooden door flew open, slamming against the wall. A cold wind blew through the room, and with it came the sound of distant, hollow breathing, like the slow exhale of something ancient.

"Let's kick rocks." Marz shouted.

Without waiting for a vote, the group bolted through the open door.

The hallway beyond the door was long and winding, with wallpaper peeling from the walls and flickering lights casting eerie shadows. Their footsteps echoed as they sprinted, the sound of the creature's breath trailing behind them like a creeping fog.

"Faster!" Jenny yelled, her sneakers squeaking on the worn floor.

Jordan clutched the book tightly, his heart pounding in his chest. They turned corner after corner, only to find the hallway stretching endlessly ahead of them. It was as if the house itself was shifting, twisting, trying to trap them.

"Where's the end?!" Ash shouted, panic rising in her voice.

Jordan flipped through the book as they ran, desperately searching for the next choice.

"The hallway splits. Do you:

- **Take the left path? (Turn to page 92)**
- **Take the right path? (Turn to page 97)"**

"Left or right?!" Jordan yelled over the noise.
"Right!" Marz shouted.
"Left!" Jenny and Ash cried in unison.
Jordan gritted his teeth and made the call.

Chapter 4:

Jordan turned the page with sweaty fingers, his heartbeat thrumming in his ears. He had gone with the majority, taking the left path, hoping it wouldn't lead them into something worse. The hallway twisted sharply as they sprinted forward, their shoes slapping against the warped floorboards.

Behind them, the sound of ragged, inhuman breathing grew louder, chasing them through the shifting corridors. Shadows along the walls seemed to writhe, whispering in voices too faint to understand, like the house was alive and enjoying the hunt.

"This hallway doesn't end." Ash shot Jordan a panicked glance. "You sure you picked the right page?"

"No," Jordan admitted. "But we're stuck with it now!"

The hallway stretched on endlessly until, suddenly, it didn't. The walls opened into a massive atrium, dimly lit by a flickering chandelier. The group skidded to a halt, panting. The air smelled stale, like an attic left sealed for decades.

They stood frozen, taking in the scene: The atrium was enormous, with a circular design. Doors lined the walls, dozens of them. Some were cracked open, while others remained tightly shut. Faded wallpaper and crooked portraits decorated the walls, and in the middle of the room stood a tall grandfather clock, its hands ticking backward.

Jordan flipped through the book frantically as the breathing sound grew closer, followed by wet slapping sounds echoing down the corridor. "Come on, come on, tell me what to do next..."

On the page, a new passage glowed with eerie clarity:

"You enter the atrium, but you are not safe. One of the doors leads to freedom, but the others will take you deeper into the labyrinth. Beware: The wrong choice will not be forgiven. Choose carefully."

Below the text were four options:

- **Door with the cracked glass. (Turn to page 103)**
- **Door with the red frame. (Turn to page 111)**
- **Door with the carved face. (Turn to page 118)**
- **Stay and investigate the clock. (Turn to page 130)**

"Clock or door?" Jordan whispered urgently.

Marz leaned over his shoulder. "Red frame sounds cool. It's probably dangerous, though."

Jenny shook her head, pacing in tight circles. "I freakin hate this. We don't know what these doors lead to."

"Clock," Ash whispered. "I don't know why, but they're always important in cartoons."

Marz rolled his eyes. "This ain't Courage the cowardly puppy."

"Might as well be." Jenny said.

Jordan turned to the group. "Final vote: red door or clock?"

Jenny hesitated, then whispered, "Clock."

Jordan nodded and turned the page.

"You approach the clock cautiously. The hands spin backward, ticking with each passing second. As you reach out to touch it, the room shifts—the clock's chimes ring out,

deafening, and the air thickens with static electricity. You feel something change, but you don't know what—until you look up."

Jordan felt his breath hitch as the book's words seemed to come alive in front of him. The grandfather clock let out a low, mournful chime that echoed through the atrium. With each ring, the room around them rippled, like a stone tossed into a pond. The air shimmered, and suddenly the doors, every single one of them slammed shut with a deafening *BANG*.

"What the hell just happened?" Marz whispered, backing away from the clock.

Ash pointed to the walls. "Look! The paintings changed."

Jordan turned, his heart skipping a beat. The portraits on the walls now depicted them, Jordan, Marz, Ash, and Jenny all standing inside the atrium, frozen in fear. But something was off. In the paintings, they looked older. And behind them, barely visible in the shadows, was the tall, hunched figure from the earlier pages.

"Yo..." Jenny whispered, her voice shaking. "It's coming."

The air turned cold, and the ragged breathing they thought they'd left behind now filled the room again. The clock chimed one final time, and with that, the tall figure stepped out of the darkness.

It was even worse up close. The creature's limbs were long and twisted, its body hunched at an unnatural angle. Its face was a blank void with no eyes or mouth, just a smooth, pale surface where features should have been. The smell that permeated the room around it was like rotting, rancid meat.

It moved slow and deliberately, as if savoring the fear radiating from the group.

"Let's go!" Marz shouted, but the doors were all shut.

"We're trapped!" Ash cried, pressing herself against the wall.

Jordan flipped the book open again, frantically searching for the next choice.

"The shadow offers you a gift. If you take it, you may escape. If you refuse, it will chase you until you are consumed by the labyrinth. Choose carefully."

Options:

- **Take the gift. (Turn to page 142)**
- **Refuse and fight. (Turn to page 150)**

Jordan's hands shook as he read the options aloud. "Well. what do we wanna do. Take the gift or fight?"

"I don't want anything from that creature!" Jenny whispered furiously. "It's a trap!"

"What if it's the only way out?" Marz asked, his voice uncertain for the first time.

Ash's eyes darted between the shadow and the book. "We can't fight that thing, can we?"

Jordan clenched his jaw. Every instinct told him to run.

"Alright," Jordan whispered. "We take the gift." Jenny looked horrified. "What?! Are you serious right now?"

"We don't have a choice!" Jordan shot back, flipping to page 142.

"The shadow extends a long, spindly hand. In its palm is a small object—a coin, blackened and worn. You take it. The moment the coin touches your hand, the figure smiles... though it has no mouth to smile with, you can still somehow see it."

Suddenly, the creature vanished, leaving behind only the sound of its hollow breath. The room grew still, the weight of the air lifting as if the house had lost interest for now.

Jordan stared down at the coin in his hand. It was ice-cold, with strange symbols carved into its surface. Symbols that matched the ones embossed on the book's cover.

"What do we do with that?" Ash whispered, eyeing the coin.

"I don't know," Jordan admitted, his voice trembling. "But I'm sure it's gonna tell us."

Before they could catch their breath, the chandelier overhead flickered, and the book's pages flipped on their own, stopping at the next set of instructions.

"The labyrinth will not let you go so easily. You must move forward. Another door has opened. Choose wisely."

A low groan echoed through the atrium as one of the doors, the one with the carved face swung open slowly, revealing only darkness beyond.

Marz exhaled. "Man, I am not having fun bro."

Jenny crossed her arms. "Well, we took the creepy coin. Might as well see where the creepy door leads." Ash gave Jordan a nervous glance. "You really think we're going to get out of here?"

Jordan slipped the coin into his pocket and held up the book. "Only one way out it seems, we keep playing."

Without another word, the group approached the door with the carved face, its wood twisted into a grotesque grin. Jordan reached out, his hands trembling, and walked through.

Chapter 5:

The darkness swallowed them whole, cold and absolute. Jordan's hand tightened around the coin in his pocket, as if the small, blackened disc could anchor him. His friends stood close, their breathing shallow and fast. The air inside the room was dense, pressing in on them like the house itself was alive and waiting to devour them.

Then, with a *thunk*, the door slammed shut behind them. Jenny jumped, stifling a scream. "Why does every door have to slam in this dumb place?"

"Because this place is an asshole," Ash whispered, hugging herself tightly. Her voice trembled, but she tried to mask it with a half-hearted shrug.

Marz clicked on his pocket flashlight, casting a thin, flickering beam into the void ahead. "Man... this just keeps getting worse my dudes."

The walls surrounding them were carved from old wood, full of grotesque faces, twisted, grinning, and sneering expressions that seemed to shift and turn away when the light hit them. Their hollow eyes followed the group as they moved deeper into the room, giving the unsettling impression that they were being watched by hundreds of unseen eyes.

"I don't like this," Jenny muttered. "Not at all."

"I don't either homegirl," Jordan whispered. "Let's keep going and hurry up and get out of here."

The book glowed faintly in Jordan's hands, its next page waiting for them. As if on cue, the text began to shimmer, a new passage forming beneath the old one.

"The carved faces mark a trial of trust and deceit. One of you will tell the truth, while the others will lie. If you make the wrong choice, the faces will not let you pass. Answer the riddle to open the next door."

Below the instructions, the text revealed a riddle:

"Two doors stand before you—one leads to freedom, the other to doom. One guardian always tells the truth; the other, only lies. You may ask one question to reveal the safe door. Choose wisely—if you fail, the labyrinth will consume you."

Marz groaned. "Great. A logic puzzle. I barely passed math class."

Ash rubbed her hands, thinking aloud. "It's a classic riddle, right? You ask something that forces a truthful answer no matter what."

Jordan nodded, grateful that at least one of them had a clue. "Okay, but I don't remember the exact solution."

Jenny crossed her arms. "Come on my dudes, we got this."

As they debated, two wooden figures stepped from the shadows, carved, puppet-like beings with blank, soulless faces. Each stood beside a door: one door painted black, the other red.

The figures bowed in unison, their wooden joints creaking. Then, in voices hollow and mechanical, they spoke:

"One of us tells the truth. One of us lies. Ask your question."

The group stood frozen, the weight of the puzzle pressing down on them. The red door seemed to hum faintly, almost inviting them in. The black door stood silent and cold.

"We only get one shot," Ash whispered. "If we mess this up we're screwed."

Jenny shot her a sly look. "We're not going to mess this up little miss worried pants."

Jordan flipped through the book's pages again, searching for any hint or clue, but the only words glowing on the page were:

"The answer lies in the question you choose."

Jordan took a deep breath. "Okay, here's the question: 'If I asked the other guardian which door leads to freedom, what would they say?'"

The wooden figures tilted their heads in unison, their joints creaking ominously.

Both guardians pointed to the Red Door. Jordan exhaled slowly. "It's the black door. That's the safe one."

Jenny narrowed her eyes. "Hold up, hold up. How do you know that?"

Jordan turned toward her, his voice steady. "It's how the riddle works. Like from the movie Labyrinth, remember? No matter who lies or tells the truth, the answer they give will always point to the wrong door. So we have to take the opposite of what they say."

Ash looked confused. "I'm not sure that makes sense."

Marz blew out a breath. "Yeah, that sounds very convoluted man."

"You don't even know what that means goober." Jenny smiled back.

With a final glance at the two guardians, Jordan placed his hand on the black door's handle. The wood was cold under his fingers, and for a moment, he hesitated, what if he was wrong? What if the next step led them straight into a trap?

"Here goes something," Jordan whispered. He twisted the handle and pulled the door open.

Beyond the threshold lay a narrow corridor, dimly lit by flickering bulbs embedded in the ceiling. The air smelled faintly of dust and mold, but it didn't feel as oppressive as the atrium had.

"This feels slightly better," Ash murmured, stepping forward cautiously.

Marz followed, casting glances over his shoulder. "If we die, I'm blaming Jordan."

Jenny lingered by the door, her arms still crossed. "This better not lead to something worse."

Jordan gave her a weak smile. "Only one way to find out."

The group stepped into the corridor, and as soon as the door shut behind them, the oppressive weight of the labyrinth seemed to ease slightly, like they'd taken one small step toward freedom.

As they walked deeper into the corridor, Jordan felt the coin in his pocket grow warmer, as if it were responding to something in the air around them. He pulled it out and examined it under Marz's flashlight beam.

The strange symbols on the coin glimmered faintly. They looked like directions, north, south, east, west.

"Dude" Jordan whispered. "I think this coin is a map."

Ash leaned closer, studying the markings. "A map to what?"

"Maybe the way out," Jordan said. "Or maybe it tells us where we are and where to go."

Marz whistled softly. "Pretty gnarly man."

Jenny squinted at the symbols. "How do we know which way to go, though?"

Jordan turned the coin over in his hand. The symbols shifted slightly, rearranging themselves until they formed a glowing arrow. The arrow pointed forward, deeper into the corridor.

"Looks like we follow the arrows," Jordan said with a grin, feeling a flicker of hope for the first time.

With the coin leading the way, the group pressed on, the air growing colder with each step. The corridor twisting and turning, branching into smaller paths that seemed to loop back on themselves. But the coin's arrow stayed steady, always pointing forward, guiding them deeper into the maze.

After what felt like hours, they reached another door. This one carved with strange runes that glowed faintly in the dark. Jordan hesitated, then flipped to the next page.

"You have found the hidden door. Inside lies the heart of the labyrinth. But beware—once you enter, there is no turning back."

Jordan looked up at his friends. "This is it. The book says there's no turning back after this."

Marz cracked his knuckles nervously. "Great. No pressure or anything."

Ash gave a playful shrug. "Let's go see what kind of fresh hell awaits us."

Jenny sighed, rolling her eyes. "Fresh hell's better than stale hell I guess."

"Your breath is stale." Marz laughed back.

Jordan took a deep breath and placed his hand on the rune-covered door. The wood pulsed beneath his palm, as if alive, and the runes glowed brighter.

"On three," Jordan whispered. "One... two..."

He pushed the door open.

Chapter 6:

The rune-covered door swung open with a low, shuddering creak, revealing a cavernous space beyond. The air was thick with the scent of old stone and damp wood, and the sound of distant whispers echoed from unseen corners. The group stepped inside cautiously, their footsteps barely making a sound on the cold floor.

A faint blue glow illuminated the vast chamber, radiating from a massive stone pedestal in the center. Above it, suspended in midair, floated an ancient mirror framed in ornate silver. The glass shimmered, its surface swirling with dark tendrils of smoke, as if reflecting something not of this world.

Jordan's stomach twisted with unease. He knew, deep down, that they were standing in the heart of the labyrinth, the point of no return. And something told him that the mirror was more than just a reflection. "This doesn't feel good," Jenny whispered, her voice brittle with fear. "Really, this feels fucked."

"You think?" Marz whispered sarcastically, though the nervous quiver in his voice betrayed him.

Ash stepped closer to the mirror, her eyes narrowing. "Maybe this is the way out."

Jordan nodded, flipping open *Endless Paths* to the next glowing passage.

"You stand before the heart of the labyrinth. The mirror holds your way out, but it will not let you go easily. You must

confront what you fear most. Beware: Reflections lie, and not all who enter will return unchanged."

Beneath the passage, two new choices appeared:

"Step into the mirror and face the truth. (Turn to page 153)

Refuse the mirror and search for another exit. (Turn to page 160)"

Jordan read the options aloud, and the group exchanged uncertain glances.

"We have to step into the mirror," Ash whispered. "That's what the book wants."

Jenny shook her head furiously. "No. No way. Mirrors are bad news. We need to find another way."

Marz's eyes locked on the swirling glass. "I hate to say it, but I think Ash is right. If the mirror is the heart of the labyrinth, it's probably the only way out."

Jordan's pulse raced as he glanced between the two choices. Every part of him wanted to turn back, to search for another door, another solution, but they'd already seen what happened when they tried to take shortcuts in the game. There was no guarantee they'd get another chance.

"Alright," Jordan said softly. "We go through the mirror."

Jenny groaned, pressing a hand to her forehead. "We're gonna die."

Jordan approached the mirror slowly, his breath fogging against the cold glass. The swirling smoke on the surface seemed to still as he drew near, reflecting his image back at him, but something was off. His reflection stared back with an eerie intensity, his eyes a little too wide, and started smiling when Jordan wasn't, and the smile unnaturally wide and sharp.

"This is stupid," Jenny whispered one last time.

Jordan took a deep breath, reached out and touched the mirror.

The glass rippled like water, swallowing his hand. For a moment, it felt like plunging into icy water, but then the sensation shifted. It wasn't just cold; it was alive. The mirror *pulled*, dragging Jordan forward, until the rest of him disappeared into the swirling void.

"Jordan!" Ash shouted.

Without hesitation, Marz grabbed Ash's hand. "Let's do this yo!"

Before Jenny could protest, Marz and Ash lunged forward, pulling her along as they all plunged into the mirror together.

The world beyond the mirror was a twisted, upside-down version of the room they had just left. Everything was distorted, the angles sharp and wrong. The pedestal was gone, replaced by a spiraling staircase that descended into endless darkness. The air was thick, heavy with the scent of iron, and strange whispers echoed from below.

Jordan landed hard on the ground, groaning as he rubbed his shoulder. Marz, Ash, and Jenny stumbled beside him, catching their breath.

"We're still alive," Marz muttered, almost in disbelief.

"Yeah, but where are we?" Ash whispered, turning in a slow circle.

Jenny's eyes widened as she looked around. "It's... it's us."

Jordan followed her gaze and saw what she meant. Reflections of themselves lined the walls, each trapped inside the glass like portraits frozen in time. Some of the reflections stared back blankly. Others looked twisted, grinning wildly or crying silently.

Jordan noticed one reflection that made his heart stop: his own image, standing perfectly still, except for its eyes. The reflected Jordan gave him a cold, knowing smile, one that didn't belong to him.

"That's not us," Jordan whispered, his blood running cold.

A passage appeared in glowing letters on the wall, written in the same script as the book:

"Only one reflection is real. To leave, you must confront it. But choose wrong, and you will take its place."

Jenny stepped back, panic rising in her voice. "What does that mean? What happens if we pick the wrong one?"

Jordan didn't answer, he didn't need to. He knew what the game was asking. One of their reflections was the true version of themselves. The version behind the mask. The version they hid from the others. If they chose wrong, they'd be trapped forever in the glass, just another warped portrait in the labyrinth's endless gallery.

"Great," Marz muttered, rubbing his face. "Another puzzle. This book seriously sucks bro."

They stood in silence, staring at their reflections. Each version of themselves seemed identical, except for the small, subtle ways they were *wrong*. Jenny's reflection blinked too often. Marz's reflection smirked like he knew a secret. Ash's image looked almost *too* calm, too serene, for the situation they were in.

Then there was Jordan's reflection. It didn't blink. It didn't move. It just smiled, cold and steady.

"That's it," Jordan whispered, his heart pounding. "That's the one."

Ash frowned. "How do you know?"

"Because..." Jordan hesitated, trying to find the right words. "Because the game has been trying to trick us the whole time. The reflections that seem *normal* are the wrong ones. The real version would never act like that."

Jenny gave him a doubtful look. "You're sure about this?"

"No," Jordan admitted. "But we have to try."

With a deep breath, he stepped forward and placed his hand on the still reflection, the one that hadn't blinked, smiled, or moved the entire time. For a moment, nothing happened. Then, with a loud *crack*, the glass shattered.

The room around them shifted violently, the walls rippling as if the entire world was coming undone. The mirror burst into shards, scattering across the floor in a cascade of shimmering glass.

A blast of cold air rushed through the room, and suddenly, they were back in the atrium. The carved faces on the walls twisted into silent screams, then crumbled to dust.

"Is that it," Ash whispered, wide-eyed. "Are we out."

The coin in Jordan's pocket grew warm again, and he pulled it out, watching as the symbols rearranged one last time. The arrow on the coin now pointed directly at the door they had entered from, except now, it glowed faintly with a soft, welcoming light.

"That's the way out," Jordan said, his voice hoarse but certain. Without hesitation, the group moved toward the glowing door. Marz threw it open, and beyond the threshold was Jordan's bedroom, just as they had left it.

They stepped through the door, and the moment they crossed the threshold, the oppressive weight of the labyrinth vanished. The air was warm again, and the sounds of the real world came rushing in, cars outside, the hum of the streetlights.

Jordan collapsed onto his bed. Marz leaned against the wall, shaking his head in disbelief.

"Okay," Marz said, grinning. "That was the dumbest thing we've ever done. And also the coolest."

Jenny sat down heavily on the floor, her face pale. "I never, ever want to see a mirror again."

Ash flopped onto the bed beside Jordan, staring at the ceiling. "I'm just glad we're alive."

Jordan smiled faintly, the coin still warm in his hand. They had made it.

Chapter 7:

For a few precious moments, the group allowed themselves to believe it was over. Jordan's room, with its familiar posters and cluttered desk, felt like an oasis of safety after the madness they had just endured. The cursed book *Endless Paths* lay on the floor, its pages now blank as if drained of all their ominous power.

"I'm never touching a book again," Jenny muttered, sprawled on the floor.

Marz, still riding the high of their escape, threw a Skittle into the air and caught it in his mouth. "I mean, come on, how many kids can say they survived a death maze? We're practically legends."

Ash rolled her eyes. "If being a legend means almost dying in a creepy mirror world, I'll pass."

Jordan sat on the edge of his bed, flipping the warm coin between his fingers. He couldn't shake the feeling that something was off. The book was supposed to be finished. They had solved the puzzle, survived the labyrinth, and made it out. But the coin in his hand still buzzed with energy, like it was waiting for something.

And that's when he noticed it.

"Dudes," Jordan said slowly, his throat dry. "Where's the book?"

Everyone froze.

Jenny sat up, her eyes wide. "It was right there."

Ash stood and checked the floor. Nothing. The spot where *Endless Paths* had landed was empty. Marz frowned, looking under the bed and around the room.

"It's gotta be here somewhere. It couldn't just disappear."

But it had. The cursed book, the very thing that had dragged them into that nightmare, was gone. Jenny's voice wavered.

Jordan rubbed the coin nervously. "I don't know how, but I don't think the game's over."

Ash's brow furrowed as she grabbed her sketchbook and flipped to one of her drawings. It was a rough sketch of the mirror from the labyrinth, jagged and eerie. She tapped the page.

"What if the mirror was just another part of the game? What if there's more?"

Marz groaned. "More? You've got to be kidding me. That was the final boss, right?"

Jordan's hand felt warm around the coin. "The book's gone, and the coin's still active. There's gotta be something else."

The room grew colder, so cold that their breath came out in puffs of mist.

The air shimmered, and slowly, a single piece of paper floated down from the ceiling, as if dropped by an invisible hand. It fluttered to the ground, landing at Jordan's feet.

He picked it up cautiously, his heart hammering in his chest. It was a page torn from *Endless Paths*, the edges jagged. Written in the same eerie script, it read:

"Congratulations, players. You have completed the first chapter. But the game is far from over. Your choices now extend beyond the book. The labyrinth has followed

you—your world is now part of the game. New challenges await."

Jenny backed away, shaking her head. "No. No, no, no. We're done man. We already finished it!"

Ash just stared at the page. "Apparently not."

Marz laughed nervously, though there was no humor in it. "Okay, this is officially nuts my bros."

Jordan dropped the page like it burned his hands. The coin in his pocket buzzed sharply, and he pulled it out. This time, the symbols on its surface rearranged into something new, an address.

"It's giving us directions," Jordan whispered. "Someplace we're supposed to go."

Jordan read the address aloud. "243 Monroe Street."

Jenny's face paled. "That's the old movie theater." Marz whistled. "The haunted movie theater of death? Great. That's just really great guys."

Jordan ran a hand through his hair, "Looks like it's where the next chapter starts."

Ash flipped back and forth through her sketchbook as if the answer were hidden in her drawings. "Do we really have to go there? What if this is all just another trick?"

Jenny crossed her arms. "We have a choice, right? We don't *have* to play."

But as soon as the words left her mouth, the coin buzzed violently, heating up in Jordan's hand. A new message appeared on the torn page, as if written by an invisible pen:

"Refusing to play will result in elimination. Elimination means death. All players must complete the game."

Jenny stumbled backward. "Oh great, that's just freakin great."

The air in the room grew thicker, the sense of impending doom creeping over them like a shadow. Jordan knew there was no way out. The game wasn't going to let them quit, not without consequences.

Marz stood, his face pale but determined. "Alright, if we're doing this, let's do it right. Redbulls, skittles and snickers bars. Better to face it head-on than sit here waiting for whatever's coming."

Jordan nodded, slipping the coin into his pocket. "We'll meet tomorrow, right after school. Bring flashlights and energy drinks"

Jenny groaned, wrapping her arms around herself. "We're really doing this, aren't we?"

Ash offered her a small, brave smile. "It's just a movie theater. What's the worst that could happen?"

As they prepared to leave, Jordan glanced back at the torn page lying on the floor. A final line of text had appeared at the bottom, written in dark, slashing letters:

"Once you enter the next chapter, there will be no turning back. Beware: Some paths lead to freedom. Others will leave you trapped—forever."

He folded the page and slipped it into his pocket with the coin. Whatever waited for them at 243 Monroe Street, they had no choice but to face it.

Chapter 8:

T he next day arrived too soon, the weight of the previous night hanging heavily over Jordan and his friends. School had passed in a blur, every bell ringing louder than usual, every hallway too narrow. By the time the final bell rang, Jordan's hands were already in his pockets, fingers fiddling with the coin.

"See you at the theater," Jordan whispered as the group split off to grab their supplies and meet up at 243 Monroe Street.

The sun was just setting when they gathered in front of the old, abandoned movie theater. The Monroe Theater was a relic of the past, a crumbling Art Deco building with cracked windows and a faded marquee that read "Coming Soon: Horror Double Feature. Friday the 13th and Nightmare on elm Street.

Marz tilted his head, staring up at the old sign. "Killer movies man."

Ash adjusted her backpack straps, gripping her sketchbook tight against her chest. "Let's get this over with."

With a groan of rusted metal, the front door creaked open on its own. "Great," Jenny muttered. "It's *expecting* us."

The group hesitated only a moment before stepping through the doorway. The air inside was stale and heavy, carrying the faint smell of old popcorn and dust.

The lobby was a decaying shrine to the past. Old posters curled at the edges inside cracked frames, their images faded beyond recognition. A tattered concession stand stood against the far wall, and the scent of stale popcorn lingered in the air, mingling with something metallic and rotten. Dust coated every surface, dulling the neon glow of a forgotten arcade machine humming faintly in the corner.

Ash paused by the arcade machine, brushing dust from its cracked screen. The lights flickered, showing glimpses of pixelated figures, a maze-like game with no exit.

"Fitting," Ash murmured, tracing a line in the dust. "It's us. We're in the game."

Jordan felt the weight of the coin in his pocket, buzzing faintly, pulling them deeper inside. "The sooner we get in, the sooner we get out," he whispered, though he wasn't sure if that was true.

"Anyone else find it odd that the power is on in this place?" Marz Whispered.

"Yeah," Jenny answered. "First thing I noticed."

The group moved cautiously toward the theater doors, passing the cracked popcorn machine. Jenny stopped in her tracks, staring inside the dusty glass.

"Jordan," she whispered, "that's not popcorn." Jordan stepped closer. Inside the machine, yellowed teeth tumbled softly against the metal tray, clinking like brittle bones.

Ash's face paled. "I hate everything about this." Before anyone could move, shuffling footsteps echoed from the far side of the lobby.

Three phantom ushers emerged from the shadows, their limbs jerking with unnatural stiffness. Their faces were blank, smooth like melted wax, yet they seemed to see perfectly without eyes. Each usher held a torn ticket stub in a skeletal hand, offering them like silent demands.

"Your seats are ready," one usher rasped, its voice crackling like a broken speaker.

"Please take your seats," hissed another, jerking its head in a grotesque bow.

Jenny backed away, her breath coming in short gasps. "We're not sitting down."

The nearest usher's face twisted into an impossible grin, splitting into three crooked mouths. "Oh, but you are."

The ushers surged forward, grabbing the kids with bony hands. Cold, skeletal fingers latched onto their wrists, dragging them toward the dark theater doors that loomed like an open maw.

"Unhand me you greasy scallywags!" Marz yelled, struggling against their grip.

Jordan twisted in their grasp, his heart pounding. But the ushers were relentless, pulling them deeper into the theater.

The double doors groaned open, revealing Theater 3. It was small, cramped, and lined with red velvet seats that reeked of mildew and dust.

Rows of decayed patrons sat silently in the seats, their hollow-eyed faces locked in expressions of terror. Their clothes were tattered relics from another time, oversized sweaters, denim jackets, and neon sneakers.

Ash shivered. "They look like they've been here forever."

As they moved through the aisles, the patrons' heads began to turn, slowly tracking them with lifeless eyes. Jordan's stomach churned.

The film projector above hummed softly, flickering to life. The screen glowed, casting a cold light across the room. Jordan's blood turned as their names appeared on the screen:

- **Jordan H.**
- **Jenny T.**
- **Marz W.**
- **Ash C.**

They stared in stunned silence as a new line of text appeared beneath the names:

"The players are seated. The game continues."

The message faded, and the screen went dark for a moment. Then a booming voice echoed through the room, coming from nowhere and everywhere at once:

"Choose your fate."

The words on the screen shifted, revealing two options:

- **"Explore the projection room. (Turn to page 175)"**
- **"Enter the basement. (Turn to page 183)"**

Jordan swallowed hard and read the choices aloud. His voice sounded small in the vast, empty theater.

Jenny groaned. "Basement? Shit no. We are not going down there."

"Yeah, I vote projection room bro," Marz added, though his tone wavered.

Ash's eyes flickered toward the dim stairwell leading to the basement. "What if it's another trick? Like the obvious scary place is actually the safe one."

Jordan glanced down at the coin, hoping for guidance. The arrow on its surface shifted, pointing toward the basement door.

"Of course it's the basement," Jenny muttered. Marz sighed. "Alright, let's do this. Basement it is. But first chug." He passed out Redbulls and everyone chugged greedily.

Jordan nodded, fully energized and turned toward the stairwell. The group descended slowly into the darkness, their flashlights barely cutting through the thick, stale air.

The steps groaned under their weight as they made their way into the basement. The air grew colder with each step, and the faint hum of the projector above faded into silence.

When they reached the bottom, they found themselves in a long, narrow hallway lined with old movie posters, but the faces on the posters had been scratched out, leaving only blank, featureless shapes.

"That's a tad bit unsettling," Marz whispered.

Jenny shuddered. "Everything about this place feels *wrong*."

Jordan held up the coin. The arrow pointed toward a door at the end of the hallway, barely visible in the gloom.

"Almost there," Jordan said, though he wasn't sure if he was trying to convince his friends or himself. They approached the door cautiously. It was marked with a hand-painted sign: "Employees Only."

Marz gave a nervous laugh. "Guess we're employees now."

Jordan reached for the handle, but before he could turn it, the door swung open on its own, revealing a dark room beyond.

Inside, the room was filled with old film reels and dusty equipment. In the center of the room stood a single, ancient film projector, aimed at a blank section of the wall. On the projector's reel was a film canister labeled: "The Last Show."

"Do we play it?" Ash whispered. Jordan's hand trembled as he flipped open the coin. The arrow had disappeared, replaced by a simple message:

"Play the film."

Marz grimaced. "Of course. What could possibly go wrong?"

With trembling hands, Jordan reached for the projector and clicked it on. The film sputtered to life, casting jittery black-and-white images onto the wall.

At first, the screen showed an empty theater, identical to the one upstairs. But then, one by one, figures began to appear in the seats, all motionless and watching the screen.

Jenny whispered. "That's us."

They watched in horror as their own reflections filled the screen, seated exactly as they had been in Theater 3. But in the film, the reflections began to change, mouths too wide, eyes turning dark and hollow. The figures on the screen began to stand up.

"They're coming here," Ash whispered.

The projector sputtered again, and the screen went black. A loud *thud* echoed from upstairs.

Jordan didn't wait. "I think that's our cue to move."

They bolted from the room, sprinting back down the hallway and up the groaning stairs. The air around them seemed to pulse with malevolent energy, the walls vibrating as if the building itself was coming alive.

They burst into the lobby just as the figures from the film, their dark, twisted reflections, emerged from the theater room.

The popcorn machine seemed to be making a fresh batch of buttered teeth, the smell was nauseating.

"RUN!" Marz yelled. The group dashed toward the front door, hearts pounding. As they reached the entrance, the twisted reflections grew closer, their hollow eyes locked on their counterparts.

Jordan grabbed the door handle and it swung open just in time. They stumbled out into the night as the door slammed shut behind them. The figures didn't follow.

As they stood outside the theater, catching their breath, Jordan pulled the coin from his pocket. The symbols shifted once more, revealing a new message:

"Chapter 2 complete. Chapter 3 begins soon."

"What was the point of that?" Ash asked.

"I don't know," Jenny said. "But it was stupid."

Jordan stared at the coin, heart hammering in his chest. There was no way to stop the game. It was coming for them one chapter at a time.

"Next time," Jenny whispered, her voice shaky, "we're not playing by the books rules."

Ash glanced at the dark theater behind them. "We might not have a choice."

Jordan held the coin tight, knowing one thing for certain: The game wasn't over.

Chapter 9:

The night air clung to Jordan's skin as the group stood frozen outside the Monroe Theater. The world around them felt wrong, as if the game's grip extended beyond the boundaries of the old building.

Jordan inspected the coin, the symbols dancing across its surface. The once-familiar arrow that had guided them before was gone. In its place, new words scrawled across the metal:

"There are no more paths. Only consequences."

"Bruh," Jordan whispered, showing the coin to the group. "The game's rules are changing."

The walk back to their neighborhood was tense, every step heavy with unease. The streetlights flickered erratically as they passed, and the usual hum of crickets and distant traffic felt eerily absent, as if the world was holding its breath.

Jenny clung to her flashlight, keeping it aimed at the sidewalk ahead. "We need to figure out what it wants from us. And why we can't just stop?"

"I don't think it's that kind of game," Ash murmured, flipping through her sketchbook again, hoping for some clue or warning hidden in her earlier drawings.

Marz lagged behind, glancing over his shoulder every few steps. "You think those shadow-things are still out here?"

"They're part of the game," Jordan replied, gripping the coin in his pocket like a lifeline. "If we keep moving, maybe they won't catch up."

Ash stopped suddenly, causing the others to bump into her. "What if the game never stops? What if it just keeps going? What is this is our new freakin reality until we d-"

"Don't say it," Jenny snapped, her voice sharp with fear. "We're going to finish this game and be just fine. Somehow."

When they finally reached Jordan's house, the porch light flickered, buzzing loudly before settling into a dim, unreliable glow. Jordan unlocked the door, and the group stepped inside, grateful for the familiar warmth of the house.

Sativa, Jordan's Rottweiler, greeted them at the door, her tail wagging cautiously. But the moment Jordan closed the door behind them, Sativa froze, her ears perked and her gaze fixed on the far corner of the living room. Jordan followed her gaze and saw the book.

Endless Paths sat neatly on the coffee table, as if it had been waiting for them. Its black cover gleamed, and a bookmark stuck out from its middle pages.

The book seemed to hum softly, almost inviting them to open it. Sativa growled low in her throat, standing between the group and the cursed object.

Marz gave a shaky laugh. "I'm starting to think this book really hates us."

Jordan approached the coffee table cautiously, Sativa growling beside him. With trembling hands, he opened the book to the bookmarked page. The text glowed faintly, written in the same unsettling script:

"The game's rules have shifted. From now on, your choices will bleed into the real world. Pay close attention: What happens in the book will happen to you and your loved ones."

Below the message, the first new choice appeared:

"There is someone waiting for you at the door. Do you let them in? (Turn to page 201)

Or do you ignore the knock? (Turn to page 208)"

The moment Jordan finished reading, a sharp, deliberate knock echoed from the front door. Everyone froze.

"No," Jenny whispered, backing into the wall. "Don't answer it."

Sativa barked, low and menacing, her hackles raised.

Marz's eyes darted between the front door and the book in Jordan's hands. "What if we ignore it? What happens then?"

Jenny shook her head. "What if ignoring it makes things worse?"

Another knock echoed through the house, louder this time, and more insistent.

Jordan looked at the others, feeling the weight of the decision pressing down on him.

"Alright, quick vote. Do we answer, or do we ignore it?"

Ash crossed her arms, frowning. "Answer. If the game's forcing us to make a choice, it might get worse if we ignore it."

Jenny shook her head violently. "No! We don't even know who or what is out there."

Marz hesitated for a second but nodded toward Ash. "I'm with Ash. If we ignore it, the game will punish us."

Jordan exhaled slow trying to push back the rising panic. His heart told him that neither option would end well.

"Alright," Jordan whispered. "We answer."

He turned to the bookmarked page, his fingers trembling as he flipped to page 201.

The moment Jordan made the choice, the front door creaked open on its own. Everyone stood frozen as a figure stepped inside, a man in a long, dark trench coat, his face partially obscured by the shadow of his wide-brimmed hat. His eyes gleamed faintly in the dim light, and a strange, unsettling smile curled across his lips.

"Good evening, players," the man said softly, his voice smooth and chilling. "I've been waiting for you."

Sativa barked fiercely, but the man didn't flinch. Instead, he tipped his hat politely toward the group.

"Who are you?" Jordan asked, his throat dry.

The man gave a slow smile. "You can call me, the Gamekeeper."

The Gamekeeper's presence filled the room with an unnatural chill. He stepped further inside, casually inspecting Jordan's living room as if he belonged there.

"The game has only just begun," he said, his voice dripping with amusement. "And I'm here to ensure you play by the rules."

Jenny swallowed hard, her voice shaky. "What happens if we stop playing?"

The Gamekeeper's smile widened. "Stopping isn't an option. You either play, or the game plays you."

Ash clutched her sketchbook tighter. "What do you want from us?"

"Ah, that," the Gamekeeper said, his gaze settling on the group. "The game wants what all games want, to be played to completion."

He reached into his coat and pulled out a second coin, identical to the one in Jordan's pocket. With a flick of his wrist, he tossed it to Jordan, who caught it instinctively.

"That's your next token," the Gamekeeper whispered. "You'll need it soon."

Before anyone could respond, the Gamekeeper tipped his hat once more. "Until next time, players."

And just like that, he turned and walked out the door, disappearing into the night as if he had never been there at all.

Jordan stared at the second coin in his hand, his mind reeling. The game had introduced a new player, and a new layer of danger. Whatever the Gamekeeper was, he wasn't just part of the book. He was something else entirely.

Jenny sat down heavily on the couch, burying her face in her hands and rubbing her temples. "We're never getting out of this are we?"

Jordan flipped the new coin over in his hand. The symbols on its surface were different from the first coin, more complex, with jagged lines and spirals that seemed to shift under the dim light.

The book on the coffee table hummed softly, as if pleased with their progress.

Chapter 10:

The night stretched on, silent and heavy, as if the whole world knew the stakes had shifted. The second coin sat in Jordan's palm, its strange symbols glowing faintly under the dim light. Sativa sat beside him, growling softly, her gaze locked on the cursed book as if she could sense it pulsing with danger.

"We need a plan," Ash said, breaking the silence. "If the rules are changing, we need to figure out how this game works."

Jenny let out a nervous laugh, slumping back into the couch. "Yeah, like a plans going to help us, we're screwed man."

Marz, sprawled on the floor with his flashlight between his fingers, tapped it nervously. "I mean, maybe the next chapter won't be that bad?"

Jordan gave him a skeptical look. "I don't know man, we've dealt with a haunted book, shadow reflections, and now some freak calling himself the Gamekeeper. Feels like it's only getting worse."

Marz shrugged. "Whatever man, don't be a wuss."

Ash flipped to a fresh page in her sketchbook. "We need to figure out what these coins mean. They have to be more than just collectibles and guides."

Jordan turned both coins over in his hand. "The first coin gave us directions. This one feels different."

The symbols on it twisted, shimmering faintly under the light.

"I think it's connected to something we haven't seen yet."

Jenny rubbed her temples. "I'm so tired of puzzles."

Ash smiled faintly, though her expression remained grim. "At least it's not another riddle. Yet."

They gathered around Jordan as he laid the two coins side by side on the coffee table. The first coin's arrow had faded, leaving only simple directional symbols. But the second coin seemed to move, the lines shifting like a living maze.

Jordan leaned closer. "These symbols, they look like a map or a code."

Ash sketched the designs quickly into her notebook, her pencil gliding across the paper. "Maybe if we line them up with something in the book..."

Sativa's growl deepened as Jordan flipped open *Endless Paths*. The book seemed to hum in response, its blank pages flickering with faint, ghostly images.

"Look!" Marz pointed. "Something's there."

The book's text reappeared slowly, as if written by an invisible hand. A new passage formed before their eyes:

"**THE SECOND TOKEN UNLOCKS** the next path. To survive, you must understand what the symbols hide. Follow the lines—but beware: Not every path leads to safety."

Below the text, two options emerged, each tied to a symbol on the second coin:

- **The spiral. (Turn to page 231)**
- **The jagged line. (Turn to page 245)**

Marz whistled softly. "So, which new hell should we pick?"

Jenny crossed her arms tightly. "I vote for the one that doesn't get us killed."

Ash tapped the spiral symbol in her sketchbook. "Spirals usually represent cycles, things repeating. Maybe it means something safer, like another maze maybe."

"Or it's another never ending trap," Jenny muttered. "Like everything else in this game."

Jordan weighed the choices in his mind. The spiral was familiar, almost comforting. But the jagged line, it felt unpredictable, like a storm waiting to hit.

"Well, we need to pick one I guess," Jordan said quietly. "Before the book does it for us."

Jordan ran a hand through his hair, glancing at the group. "We go with the jagged line."

Jenny groaned. "Of course we do, I mean, what could go wrong with a jagged gnarly looking line."

Marz chuckled nervously. "Well, if we die, at least we die doing something cool."

Ash gave Jordan a small nod. "Jagged line it is."

With a deep breath, Jordan turned to page 245.

"The jagged path is a dangerous one. It twists and breaks, testing your every step. But those who survive it may find something greater: the truth hidden at the game's heart."

As Jordan read the words aloud, the lights in the room flickered violently. The air grew heavy, the lights grew dim, and a low rumbling sound echoed through the walls, as if the house itself was groaning in protest.

The room shifted. Before any of them could react, the ground seemed to vanish beneath their feet. The world twisted and bent, and the group was pulled into the book, dragged through its pages like ink spilling across a canvas.

Jordan hit the ground hard, the wind knocked out of him. Around him, the others landed with groans and gasps, struggling to their feet.

They weren't in Jordan's house anymore. They stood in the middle of a strange, dark forest, the twisted trees towering overhead.

The ground beneath them was uneven, crisscrossed with jagged lines that seemed to glow faintly, forming a path that stretched endlessly in both directions.

"Great," Jenny whispered, her voice trembling. "This is just freakin great."

"Yep," Ash said quietly, brushing dirt from her hands. "We're in the damn book."

Marz groaned, rubbing his shoulder. "We should've picked the damn spiral bro."

Jordan held up the second coin, which now burned hot in his palm. The glowing lines on the ground matched the symbols on the coin exactly.

"I guess we follow the path," Jordan said, his voice steady. "Seems like the only way forward."

The group trudged along the glowing path, the forest pressing in around them. Shadows flickered between the trees, and strange whispers floated through the air, words just beyond understanding.

Ash stayed close to Jordan, sketching the twisted forest as they walked. "This place feels alive."

"It probably is," Marz muttered, kicking a stone off the path.

Jenny hugged herself, glancing nervously at the shadows. "I really don't like this. Like, at all."

As they rounded a bend in the path, the forest opened up to reveal a massive clearing. In the center of the clearing stood a stone archway, its surface covered in the same shifting symbols as the second coin. Jordan held the coin up, and the symbols on the arch began to glow.

"This is it," Jordan whispered. "The way forward."

Just as the group approached the archway, a new message appeared, scrawled across the stone in glowing letters:

"Once you pass through, there is no going back. Choose carefully."

Jenny groaned. "Why does everything in this game come with a damn ominous warning?"

Marz gave a nervous laugh. "Because it's a terrible game."

Ash tilted her head, studying the symbols. "We don't have much of a choice. If we don't move forward..."

"The game moves for us," Jordan finished grimly.

Without another word, he stepped toward the archway, the coin buzzing in his hand. The symbols glowed brighter, and the air hummed with energy.

"Together," Jordan whispered. "We go through together."

The group exchanged tense glances, then stepped through the archway as one.

The moment they passed through the archway, the forest vanished. The world twisted again, and they found themselves standing on the edge of a massive cliff, overlooking a swirling void of shadows below.

A narrow bridge stretched across the void, leading to another archway on the far side.

Jordan's heart pounded. "Well, we have to cross."

Jenny shook her head. "No way. Dude that bridge is barely holding together."

"It's the only way forward," Ash whispered, her voice steady.

Marz groaned. "I told ya, we should have picked the damn spiral."

Jordan gripped the coin tightly, feeling the weight of the game pressing down on him. "We should stick together. No one falls behind. Hold hands you love birds, let's do this."

With that, they stepped onto the bridge, the planks creaking ominously beneath their weight.

Chapter 11:

The narrow bridge stretched over the endless abyss of swirling shadows. Each step they took felt like a gamble, the rotting planks groaning under their weight. The symbols on the second coin glowed softly in Jordan's hand, guiding them forward. But the bridge seemed impossibly long, as if the destination on the other side kept shifting and stretching out of reach.

"Just don't look down," Marz muttered, gripping the hand rope so tightly his knuckles turned white.

Jenny shot him a withering look. "Why do you people always say that? As if that makes it better."

"Whoa, What'dya mean, you people?" Marz threw back.

Jenny just shook her head with a slight smile. "Shut up Goob."

Ash stayed close to Jordan, her hand clenching the strap of her sketchbook like a lifeline.

"Something feels weird," she whispered, her eyes flicking toward the shadows below. "Like we're being watched."

Jordan tightened his grip on the coins in his pocket. "I feel it too, let's just keep moving. Whatever's waiting for us we..."

The bridge shook violently, cutting him off mid-sentence. Jenny let out a small scream as the planks beneath her feet shifted dangerously.

"Hurry up, run!" Ash shouted.

Just as they surged forward, the shadows began to rise from the abyss like curling tendrils of smoke, slithering toward the bridge. The tendrils of darkness gathered ahead of them, coiling and twisting until they took shape, human shapes, mirroring Jordan, Ash, Marz, and Jenny. The figures flickered, their faces distorted like corrupted reflections in a broken mirror.

"Not this shit again man." Marz whispered, his voice barely audible. "Why are they us?"

Jenny backed away slowly, her breath coming in shallow gasps. "Just like the freaks from the theater."

"These feel like more than reflections.," Jordan said quietly. "They look solid."

The shadow figures smiled, their mouths stretching wide, their movements jerky and unnatural. Then, without warning, they lunged.

"Run!" Jordan shouted, grabbing Ash's arm and sprinting forward. The others followed, their footsteps thundering on the fragile planks. The shadow versions of themselves pursued them, gliding effortlessly across the bridge, their twisted smiles never wavering.

Planks splintered underfoot, the entire bridge shuddering as if ready to collapse. Jenny stumbled but caught herself, glancing back just in time to see her shadow self gaining on her. "Go, go!" Marz yelled, pulling her forward.

"We're not going to make it!" Ash cried, her voice full of panic.

Jordan glanced down at the glowing coin in his hand. The symbols twisted, rearranging into a new message:

"Only one path forward. One must fall."

Jordan's stomach dropped as the words burned into his mind. Someone had to fall. The bridge trembled violently again, cracks splintering through the wood. The shadows drew closer, their grinning faces inches away from the group. Jenny gasped, realizing what the coin's message meant.

"It says one of us has to fall."

"Nah, fuck that." Jenny said. "Nobody's falling nowhere."

"Just keep going, nobody's falling here!" Marz shouted, looking desperately around.

The bridge groaned loudly, splitting apart. There wasn't time. Jordan's mind raced. If one of them didn't fall, none of them would make it.

Without thinking, Ash stepped forward, her expression calm and resigned.

"Ash, no." Jordan shouted, reaching for her.

But Ash just gave him a small, sad smile. "It's the only way. If I fall, the bridge will hold. See you guys around."

Before anyone could stop her, she turned and let herself fall over the edge of the bridge in a peaceful swan dive into the abyss.

Her body disappeared into the swirling shadows below, the tendrils consuming her like smoke.

"Ash!" Jenny screamed, her voice breaking.

Marz stared in horror, frozen in place. "Ash...Why man?"

Jordan felt his chest tighten, every instinct screaming at him to jump after her. But the coin in his pocket buzzed sharply, as if warning him to keep moving.

The moment Ash fell, the bridge stabilized. The splintering wood knit itself back together, the trembling ceased, and the shadow figures evaporated, disappearing into the abyss.

"We have to go," Jordan whispered, though his heart felt like it was breaking. "Ash just gave us a chance. We can't waste it."

Jenny wiped tears from her face, nodding numbly. Marz gave one last glance toward the swirling shadows below, his expression hollow, before following the others across the bridge. They ran the rest of the way in a silent daze, the weight of Ash's sacrifice pressing down on them like a lead blanket.

The group finally reached the other side of the bridge, stumbling into a wide, open field bathed in eerie moonlight. For a moment, they stood in stunned silence, trying to catch their breath.

"She's gone," Jenny whispered, hugging herself tightly. "Ash is fucking gone."

Jordan stared down at the glowing coin in his hand, guilt gnawing at him. "She didn't have to—"

"Yes, she did man, someone had to. She was the only one with the balls to do it." Marz interrupted quietly. "The game was never going to let all of us cross. Ash is a fucking gangster."

A cold wind swept across the field, carrying with it the distant sound of whispering voices, Ash's voice was among them.

"She's still here," Jordan whispered, gripping the coin tightly. "Somehow, she's still part of the game."

The coin buzzed again, and new symbols appeared on its surface. This time, they rearranged into a message:

"The fallen are never truly lost. They wait at the heart of the game."

"What does that mean?" Jenny asked, her voice shaky with a hint of hope.

Marz frowned. "I guess that's where we're supposed to go next?"

Jordan nodded slowly. "Maybe we can get Ash back if we can find it."

Jenny wiped her eyes, determination flickering behind her grief. "Then let's finish this shit. Imma shove my whole damn foot in that gamemaster dudes ass when I see him again."

Marz gave an amused nod. "I'll teabag him when you're done."

Jordan turned toward the path ahead, gripping the coin tightly. The next chapter was waiting, and this time, they wouldn't lose anyone else.

Chapter 12:

The path stretched before them, bathed in cold moonlight, leading deeper into the unknown. Jordan, Jenny, and Marz trudged forward in silence, their hearts heavy with grief over Ash's sacrifice. The glow of the second coin guided them like a distant lighthouse, its strange symbols rearranging every few minutes, reminding them that the game's next step was always just ahead.

Ash's voice echoed faintly in Jordan's mind, slipping between the whispering wind and the rustling leaves. She wasn't truly gone, not yet.

"We'll find you Ash," Jordan whispered into the wind, gripping the coin tightly. "I'm not leaving you here."

Jenny glanced over at him, her face pale and drawn. "Do you think we can really save her?"

Marz, walking beside them, shook his head. "I don't know man. This game doesn't seem like the kind that gives second chances."

Jordan held up the coin, watching its glow shift again. "Fuck giving, we'll just take one."

After what felt like hours of walking, the path opened up into what looked eerily like their neighborhood, but everything was wrong. The streets were empty, the houses stood in perfect silence, and the sky overhead shimmered with unnatural hues of purple and black.

"Great," Jenny whispered. "We're in bizarro world now."

Marz kicked a rock along the sidewalk, his expression dark. "Maybe we can find some Redbulls and Skittles while we're here."

Jordan felt a chill crawl up his spine. The world was too still. No dogs barking, no distant hum of cars, just the sound of their footsteps on the cracked pavement that seemed to be echoing off of some unseen wall above them in the sky. It was like walking through a dream where every detail was almost, but not quite, right.

As they passed what should've been Jenny's house, she stopped abruptly, staring up at the windows. "Do you see that?" she whispered.

Jordan followed her gaze and froze. In the upstairs window, Jenny's reflection stared back at them. It smiled slowly, its teeth sharp and jagged.

"Keep moving," Jordan urged, pulling Jenny away. "It's just trying to mess with us."

The second coin buzzed in Jordan's hand, growing warmer. He stopped walking, holding it up to inspect the symbols as they rearranged into a new message:

"To reach the heart, you must play one final game. Look to the places you know, but beware: Not every door leads forward."

Marz groaned. "Come on man, why all this confusing mumbo jumbo?"

Jenny crossed her arms tightly. "Because it's stupid."

Jordan glanced around, his gaze landing on a familiar sight. Sandy's old convenience store, one of their usual hangouts. Its neon sign flickered dimly, casting eerie green light onto the empty street.

"The heart of the game is here," Jordan whispered. "It's hiding in places we know."

Jenny eyed the darkened store warily. "Soooo, we just walk in and hope it doesn't eat us?"

"Pretty much," Marz muttered, flicking his flashlight on. "Redbulls on me."

The bell above the door jingled as they entered, though the sound was warped and high-pitched, like an echo. The aisles were lined with shelves, but the products were all wrong. Instead of snacks and soda, the shelves were filled with things from their memories, Jenny's old baseball glove, Marz's BMX helmet, and even a half-burned notebook from Jordan's childhood.

"Freaking weird," Marz muttered, picking up the helmet and turning it over in his hands.

Jenny backed away from a shelf displaying one of her old diaries. "I hate this man. It's like the game knows everything about us."

Jordan moved toward the back of the store, where the freezer section hummed quietly. But instead of frozen goods, the freezers held rows of books, all identical copies of *Endless Paths*, their black covers gleaming under the flickering lights.

"Maybe we need to find the right one," Jordan whispered. He pulled out the glowing coin, and its symbols rearranged into a final clue:

"The book with the missing page holds the key. Only one is real."

Marz groaned. "Of course it's another puzzle. Look at this." Marz said pointing to a cooler. "Instead of Redbulls it has Bluecows." He laughed, "Ridiculous bro."

Jenny scanned the rows of identical books, her frustration bubbling over. "How are we supposed to know which one is missing a page? There's gotta be a hundred of them."

Jordan opened one book after another, flipping through the pages as quickly as he could. Each copy seemed identical, until he reached the fifteenth book. His heart skipped a beat. One of the pages was torn out. "This is it," Jordan whispered, holding up the book.

But the moment he touched the missing pages spot, the freezer doors slammed shut, and the lights flickered violently. A deep, rumbling growl echoed from somewhere inside the store.

"Damnit man." Marz whispered, his voice tight with fear.

From the shadows between the aisles, a familiar figure stepped forward, the Gamekeeper, his wide-brimmed hat casting a long shadow over his face.

"Well done," the Gamekeeper purred, his voice smooth and sinister. "You've made it this far. But the real question is: Are you willing to do what it takes to finish?"

Jordan held the book tightly, his heart racing. "What do you mean?"

The Gamekeeper smiled, a cold, unnatural grin. "The missing page you seek... belongs to your friend. If you want to end the game, you'll need to bring her back, but not without a cost."

Jenny's eyes widened. "You can bring her back?"

"Oh, I can," the Gamekeeper whispered. "But everything in this game comes with a price."

Marz stepped forward, his jaw popping. "What kind of price?"

The Gamekeeper's grin widened. "One of you must stay behind. Forever."

The room seemed to shrink as the weight of the Gamekeeper's words settled over them. One of them had to stay, trapped inside the game, just like Ash.

"No," Jenny whispered, shaking her head. "There's gotta be another way."

"There isn't," the Gamekeeper said softly. "Choose wisely, or the game will make the choice for you."

"How about I choose my foot in your ass?" Jenny yelled.

Jordan clenched his jaw, his mind racing. There was no way they could leave anyone behind. But if they didn't make a decision, the game would do it for them.

"I'll do it," Marz said suddenly, his voice quiet but steady. "Fuck it, I'll stay."

Jordan turned to him, his heart sinking. "Marz, no."

"It's okay," Marz whispered, forcing a grin. "You guys need to get out of here. Finish this."

Before anyone could stop him, Marz reached for the Gamekeeper's hand. The shadows swirled around him, and he gave one last, crooked grin before vanishing into the darkness.

The Gamekeeper tipped his hat. "The choice has been made. The game is complete, for now."

The store dissolved into shadows, and the group was pulled back into the real world, landing hard on the sidewalk outside.

But Marz was gone.

Chapter 13:

The silence on the sidewalk was suffocating. The neon glow of the old store flickered once and then snuffed out entirely, leaving Jordan, Jenny, and the memory of Marz standing in the still night air.

"Marz..." Jenny whispered, her voice trembling. "Why man?"

Jordan gripped the second coin, now cold and lifeless, in his hand. The glowing symbols had vanished, replaced by a blank, blackened surface. The game had taken its price and now it seemed to be over.

Ash was still lost, and now Marz was gone, too. Two friends lost to a game that didn't play fair.

"We shouldn't have let him go," Jenny said, hugging herself tightly. "There has to be something we can do, a way to bring them back."

Jordan stared at the closed book tucked under his arm. *Endless Paths* was quiet now, the pages no longer shifting or glowing.

As they stood in stunned silence, a low, familiar whisper drifted on the breeze. It was soft at first, barely audible, but it grew stronger with each passing second. "Jordan... Jenny..."

Jenny froze. "That's... Marz."

Jordan's heart raced. The voice wasn't coming from the book or the coin, it was coming from somewhere else entirely.

"The heart of the game…" Jordan whispered, the realization hitting him hard. "Marz is still in there somewhere. We can still save him."

Jenny shook her head, tears welling in her eyes. "How? The Gamekeeper said—"

"Fuck the Gamekeeper," Jordan interrupted. "We're not leaving them behind."

The coin in Jordan's hand buzzed softly, as if responding to his determination. Slowly, the symbols on its surface began to reappear, shifting and rearranging into one final message:

"The final path is hidden in the beginning."

Jordan flipped through *Endless Paths*, his hands trembling. The book's pages seemed ordinary now, but he knew the answer had to be buried somewhere inside. He stopped on the first page, where the game had all began.

Beneath the familiar opening text, a new line shimmered into view:

"To reclaim what is lost, one must rewrite the final page."

Jordan's pulse quickened. "We can rewrite it. We can change the ending."

Jenny frowned. "How? The game doesn't exactly let us cheat."

Jordan grabbed a pen from his backpack, flipping to the last blank page in the book. "It's not cheating if we finish the story."

Jordan's hand shook as he pressed the pen to the page. Jenny stood beside him, watching in nervous silence. "Are you sure this will work?" she whispered.

Jordan took a deep breath. "No. But it's the only chance we've got."

He began to write:

"The players stood at the edge of the game, tired and afraid, but they refused to leave anyone behind. They rewrote the rules, breaking the cycle, and pulled their friends back into the light. The game had no choice but to let them go—together."

The moment the final word hit the page, the book glowed fiercely, and the air around them trembled as if the world itself was shifting.

The night sky rippled like the surface of a pond, and a brilliant flash of light engulfed the sidewalk. Jordan and Jenny shielded their eyes as the book shuddered violently, the cover snapping shut with a resounding *clap*.

Jordan opened his eyes. Marz and Ash stood in front of them, dazed but alive.

"You did it," Ash whispered, her voice thick with disbelief. "You actually did it."

Marz blinked, looking around in confusion. "Wait... I'm not trapped?"

"Nope," Jordan grinned, his heart soaring. "We broke the game."

Jenny threw her arms around Ash, tears spilling freely down her cheeks.

Marz clapped Jordan on the back, his grin wide and genuine. "Dude. I can't believe you just rewrote the rules. That was awesome."

Just as relief washed over the group, the coin in Jordan's pocket buzzed one last time. He pulled it out, and a final message appeared on its surface:

"You've won—for now. But games never truly end."

With a swoosh the Gamekeeper was standing before them. "Well done." he said with a tip of his hat and a bow. "You've done what most have never done."

"You're a sick dude." Ash said.

He just laughed. "Aren't we all in our own little ways?"

"No." Marz said. "We don't go around killing and kidnapping little kids."

"Killing? Kidnapping? Why child, we were just playing a game, nobody has been kidnapped or killed. This was merely a fun choose your own adventure game played in real time with real feeling stakes."

"So, are you saying nothing bad was ever going to happen to us?" Jordan asked.

"Goodness no," the Gamekeeper said. "What would be the fun in that?"

"So all the imminent death and scary stay in the game forever stuff?." Ash asked, brushing a stray hair from her face.

"Just a little atmospheric tension built into the game." He replied. "We feel adding a little weight to the outcome gives a little flavor to the overall playing experience."

Marz laughed. "Sick dude. Definitely sick, but fun."

"Fun indeed." The Gamekeeper said.

"So what's next? Ash asked. "Can we play again?"

"Unfortunately not, only one game per person. Besides, once you realized there's no real danger to the game, it kind of loses its charm."

"How is any of this possible anyhow?" Jenny asks.

"Magic my dear." The Gamekeeper smiled. "There's still plenty of magic left in this world, you just have to know where to look."

"So what now?" Jordan asked.

"Now you go on with your lives." The Gamekeeper smiled. "Only now you go on with the knowledge that there's a little something extra out there. Something to keep things interesting. A little something to take the edge off, if you will."

"Oh I will," Jordan said. "I most definitely will."

The Gamekeeper smiled. "I knew you would." He tipped his hat. "Good day to you lovely people, I hope your lives are full of love, life and magic."

And with that he poofed into mist and vanished into the air.

They walked home together in silence, the weight of the ordeal slowly lifting from their shoulders. The streets were quiet, the houses familiar and warm in the glow of the streetlights.

As they reached Jordan's front porch, Marz gave him a grin. "So, uh, next adventure, we stick to Skyrim or Red Dead?"

Jordan laughed. "Yeah man, I'm dome with the choose your own adventure books for awhile."

Ash gave them a playful shove. "How about we just stick to playing hide and go find yourself."

Jenny sighed. "Hide and go find your butt." The group exchanged weary but triumphant smiles, grateful to be back where they belonged, together.

And somewhere out there, a kid was picking up a dusty old book he just found in the dark corners of some old bookshop nobody ever visits.

Opening the paged he sees the words appear. **"Endless Paths: A Game of Choices"**

And so the game begins again.

Also by B. Humphrey

Bigfoot Vs
Bigfoot Vs Werewolves
Bigfoot Vs Vampires
Bigfoot Vs Aliens
Bigfoot Vs Yeti
Bigfoot Vs Werebear
Bigfoot Vs Mothman
Bigfoot Vs The Kandahar Giant
Bigfoot Vs Chimera
Bigfoot Vs Loch Ness Monster
Bigfoot Vs Wendigo
The Great Cryptid Wars
The Moon Curse Saga
Bigfoot Vs: The Collector's Edition Books 1-10

Retro Horrors: The Lost Decade
Cassette Ghosts
Summer of the Black Star
The Arcade Incident

Dead End Drive – In
The Polaroid Project
Endless Paths: The Choose-Your-Own Doom Chronicles
Neon Dreams
The Forgotten Carnival
Satanic Panic
Skin of the Moon

Roxy Kane
A God in Chains

Sporefall
Sporefall

The Autumn Folklore Chronicles
The Forest Of Forgotten Names
The Witch Of Windspindle Hollow
The Burrowfolk Chronicles

The Fall Of America
The Final Directive

The Phantom Finders Club
A Haunting On Maplewood Street
The Secrets Of Old Fort Tower
Ghosts OF The Infirmary

The Saturn Outlaws
The Saturn Outlaws: Sky-Bandits of the Void Frontier

The Starling Sleuths
Detective Starling vol. 1
Detective Starling Vol. 2

Winter Horrors
Whispers of the Wendigo
Cold Cuts
The Dark Beneath

Standalone
The Witch of Blackwood Hollow
The Storied Mind
The Great Cryptid Wars
Chronicles of the Hairy Kind: A Field Log by Thaddeus Grieve